Off the Rim

Off the Rim

by Fred Bowen

Illustrated by
Ann Barrow

PEACHTREE

ATLANTA

Other books by Fred Bowen
T.J.'S SECRET PITCH
THE GOLDEN GLOVE
THE KID COACH
PLAYOFF DREAMS
FULL COURT FEVER

A Peachtree Junior Publication
Published by
PEACHTREE PUBLISHERS, LTD.
494 Armour Circle NE
Atlanta, Georgia 30324

Text © 1998 by Fred Bowen
Illustrations © 1998 by Ann G. Barrow

Photo of Iowa State University women's basketball practice reprinted with permission of Iowa State
University Library/University Archives.

Photo of the 1968 women's high school championship game reprinted with permission of the
Iowa Girls High School Athletic Union.

Jacket illustration by Ann G. Barrow
Book design by Loraine M. Balcsik
Composition by Dana Celentano and Dana L. Laurent

Manufactured in the United States of America
10 9 8 7 6 5 4 3 2 1
First Edition

Library of Congress Cataloging-in-Publication Data
Bowen, Fred.
    Off the rim / by Fred Bowen ; illustrated by Ann Barrow. –1st ed.
        p. cm. –(The AllStar sportstory)
        Summary: Unhappy with his inability to score for his middle school basketball team,
Chris takes lessons from his friend Greta's mother, who played in high school, and develops a
good sense of teamwork.
    ISBN 1-56145-161-4
    [1. Basketball–Fiction.] I. Barrow, Ann, ill. II. Title. III. Series:
    Bowen, Fred. AllStar sportstory.
    PZ7.B67240f 1998
    [Fic]–dc21   98-20967
                                                            CIP
                                                            AC

To Margaret Quinlin,
Stephanie Thomas,
and all my friends
at Peachtree Publishers
who gave me my first shot.

ONE

"Three...two...one..."

Chris Skallerup could hear the countdown as he went up for his jump shot.

The instant the ball left his hand, Chris knew the shot was off. The basketball smacked against the back of the rim and spun away.

"Halftime!" laughed Greta "Gretzky" Pemberton, the star of the middle school girls' team, as she stood in the bright sun on the basketball court at Green Street Park.

"You're as bad as me," said Jason Chun, Chris's teammate on the middle school boys' team.

"That shot was a brick," Greta teased. "You've got no jumper."

"I know. That's why I'm at the end of the bench with Jason," Chris said.

"Let me try," Greta said, grabbing the ball and dribbling it between her legs.

"Okay," Chris said. "Jason and I will count you down."

As the boys started the count, Greta whipped a dribble behind her back, her blond ponytail flying.

"Three...two..."

At the count of "one," she flipped up a soft jumper. The ball sailed in a perfect arc to the basket. *Swish*. Nothing but net.

"Game." Greta beamed. "You want to try, Jason? Chris and I can count you down."

Jason shook his head. "Nah, let's play something else."

"How about me against you two guys," Greta suggested as she sank another shot.

"Those aren't fair teams," Chris said.

"For who?" Greta asked.

"How about some kind of shooting game, like H-o-r-s-e or something?" Jason asked.

Chris shook his head as another one of his shots bounced off the rim. "I stink at shooting. Mingo can shoot better than me," Chris said, looking over at Greta's black Labrador lying on the grass happily gnawing a tattered tennis ball.

"I don't know," said Jason. "It looks like Mingo would rather eat a ball than shoot it."

"Come on, let's play a game," insisted Greta.

"All right, all right," said Chris. "But not H-o-r-s-e. Jason and I can't do all of those fancy shots you do."

"Okay. How about Around the World?" Greta suggested.

"I don't know. I haven't played that game in a long time," Jason said.

"It's easy," Greta said. "It'll all come back to you. You just take a shot from six different places on the court, starting underneath the basket. Then you go to the left corner, left wing, foul line, right wing, and right corner."

"How far out?" Chris asked.

"Fifteen to eighteen feet," Greta said. "If you make your shot, you go on to the next shot. If you miss, you can either stay at your spot or take a second shot. If you hit the second shot, you move on."

"And what if you miss your second shot? You've gotta go all the way back to the beginning?" Chris asked.

"Yeah," said Jason, remembering. "And the first player who goes all the way around and back again gets 'around the world' and wins, right?"

"Right." Greta passed Jason the ball. "Why don't you start?"

Jason hit his first three shots, but his shot from the foul line fell short.

"You gonna chance it?" Greta asked, passing him the ball.

Jason eyed the rim and then passed the ball to Chris. "Nah," he decided. "I'll stick."

Chris spun his first shot in from under the basket and headed for the left corner. Standing about fifteen feet from the basket, Chris bounced the ball once, studied the rim, and took a shot. The ball glanced off the back rim and landed in Greta's hands.

"Are you gonna chance it or are you gonna stick?" she asked, getting ready to toss him the ball.

Chris held out his hands. "I'll chance it," he said. Then he took a deep breath, dipped, and pushed the ball up and away. It was headed straight for the basket but banged off the front rim and onto the blacktop. "Man, I'm the worst," he said, stomping his foot on the court.

"Shake it off," said Greta, as she reached out and caught the ball on the bounce. "My turn." Her first shot from underneath the basket fell through the net. Then she grabbed the ball, dribbled to the left corner, whirled around, and sent a perfect jump shot spinning to the hoop. *Swish.*

Greta was unstoppable. She moved quickly around the court, sinking shot after shot.

"Hey, Gretzky," Chris said. "How about a rule that your shots don't count if they touch the rim?"

Greta laughed. "And yours count only if they do?"

"That's not a bad idea," said Chris, smiling. "At least I'd have a chance of winning."

Greta took another shot and it fell easily through the net. Chris's smile melted. *Doesn't she even know how to miss?* he wondered.

At last, Greta stood deep in the left corner of the court and lofted her final shot at the basket. She stared wide-eyed as the ball nudged the front rim, bounced off the back, and rattled out.

Jason got the rebound, dribbled to the foul line, and got ready to shoot. "It's about time you gave us a chance," he said.

"Give me the ball," Greta demanded, still standing in the corner.

"You're not going to chance it, are you?" Chris asked in disbelief. "You've only got one shot left."

"Give me the ball," Greta said impatiently.

"Okay, but if you miss, you've got to go all the way back to the beginning," Chris warned as Jason tossed her the ball.

"I'm not gonna miss," she said as she flicked a quick jumper to the hoop. The shot sailed sure and straight. *Swish.*

"Game!" said Greta.

"Oh no," said Chris. "I never even got past the first shot."

"Want to play again?" Greta asked with a superior smile.

"Nah, I'd better get going," said Chris, picking his jacket up off the ground. "I'm sick of getting beat, anyway."

"Come on, you can't win if you don't play," Greta

*"I'm not gonna miss," she said as she flicked a
quick jumper to the hoop.*

reminded Chris. As always, Greta was looking for another game.

"Wrong!" Chris said with a laugh. "I can't win if I *do* play. This way I'm just cutting my losses."

"Hey, you can't go yet—you missed your last shot," said Greta. "Remember, the last shot you take has got to go in." And she tossed the ball to Chris.

Chris dropped his jacket and took the pass from Greta.

"Don't try any long shots. We don't have all night," Jason teased.

Chris touched an easy layup off the backboard and through the net. "See you later," he called as he ran up the hill toward home.

TWO

"Is that you, Christopher?" his mother called as Chris slammed the door behind him.

"Yeah, it's me," Chris answered.

"Wash your hands and set the table. Dad is picking up Anna at her volleyball game. They should be home soon."

Chris was putting plates around the table when his father and sister came through the door. "Hey, how did your team do?" Chris asked.

"We won in straight sets," Anna answered proudly. "15–12, 15–8, 15–7."

"Did you get any spikes?" Chris asked as he pretended to spike the plate in his hand across the dining room table.

Anna rolled her eyes. "No, dummy," she said. "I keep telling you, I'm a setter. Sarah and Tamika do most of the spiking for the team. My job is to get the ball up in the air close to the net so they can smash it over."

Chris's father put his arm around his daughter.

"Anna, you did a great job. I don't think they could've won without you."

"Why not?" asked Chris, not missing a chance to needle his sister. "She doesn't do much. She just pokes the ball in the air. Sarah and Tamika do all the real work."

"At least I get to play," Anna replied sharply. "Not like some other people around here."

Chris made a face and stuck out his tongue at his older sister just as his mother walked into the room.

"Oh, come on, you two," she said. "Can't you get along even for two minutes? Now let's all be pleasant and have a nice dinner. Chris, please finish pouring water for everyone. Anna, get the casserole off the counter, please. Use pot holders—it's still warm."

His mother then leaned over and lit the two tall candles on the table. His mother insisted on candles and cloth napkins every evening, even if they were having pizza for dinner. She also insisted on proper manners, so Chris took his cloth napkin and placed it across his lap, even though he really wanted to scrunch it up and throw it at his sister.

"Well, how was your day, Christopher?" his father asked.

"Okay, I guess."

"Anything interesting happen in school today?"

"Nah, same old stuff."

Chris suspiciously inspected his steaming casserole. "Does this have any onions in it?" he asked his mom as he poked at his food with his fork.

"Just a few, for flavor," she said. "I thought you didn't mind onions."

"I thought I did," Chris said under his breath, wrinkling his nose at a sliver of limp onion dangling on the end of his fork.

His father rolled his eyes and changed the subject. "Did you have basketball practice today?"

"No, our next practice is tomorrow after school," Chris answered as he dropped the onion sliver on the side of his plate and carefully picked through the rest of his food. "But I played some hoops down at Green Street Park."

"Who was there?" his mother asked.

"Just Jason, Greta, and me."

"Greta's a pretty good basketball player, isn't she?" his mother asked.

"She's awesome," Chris said. "She scores about twenty-five points a game for the girls' team."

"How's your jump shot coming?" his father asked.

Chris stared at his food. His mind was full of missed shots and limp onions. "Okay, I guess," he said.

"Do you think Coach Anderson will start playing you a bit more in the games?" his mother asked gently.

"I sure wish he would," Chris said as he pushed

around the food on his plate to make it look like he had eaten more than he had. "But I don't think he will unless I start sinking some jump shots."

"Well, keep practicing," his father said.

Anna didn't want to miss a chance to bug her brother. "Maybe Greta can help you with your jump shot," she said with a big fake smile.

Chris narrowed his eyes at his sister and was about to say something mean when he heard his mother clear her throat. He glanced quickly over at his mom and saw that she was looking straight at him. Chris decided to hold his tongue.

After dinner Chris started upstairs to do his homework.

"Remember to take your clean laundry upstairs, Christopher," his mother called.

"Where is it?" he asked.

"On the stairs."

Chris looked down and, sure enough, there on the stairs was a stack of neatly folded pants and shirts, topped by a pile of white socks rolled up like tennis balls. He gathered up his clean laundry, took it upstairs, and dumped it on his bed. He stopped for a moment and looked around his room at all the basketball posters taped to the walls. Scottie Pippen. Grant Hill. Glen Rice. Karl "The Mailman" Malone. "Hakeem the Dream." The superstars. The scorers.

Chris grabbed a rolled-up sock and tossed it toward the curtain rod above his window. The sock bumped lightly against the wall and fell behind the rod.

"It's good!" Chris said out loud. Then he started moving around the room, sending shot after shot at the curtain rod. "Basket!" he yelled every time he saw the sock slip behind the rod. His mother poked her head in the room and asked, "Christopher, what are you doing?"

Chris turned red. "Um, I'm just sorta messing around."

"Well, stop messing around and put your laundry away and get to your homework. If you've got any Spanish homework, I can help you with it in a few minutes."

"I don't have any Spanish tonight."

"Then start doing your other assignments," she said. Then she smiled. "And stop worrying about your jump shot."

Chris smiled back as she closed the door. Chris looked at the rolled-up sock in his hand and flipped one last shot at the curtain rod. The sock bounced off the rod and plopped sadly to the floor.

THREE

Phweeet!

Coach Anderson's whistle shrieked through the gym just as Chris went in for a layup. "All right, Eagles," Coach Anderson called out to his team. "Good work on the drills. It's scrimmage time." The coach's announcement brought cheers from the ten members of the Oak View Eagles basketball team.

"All right!"

"Let's play ball!"

Coach Anderson shouted out instructions. "The first string, Dontae Taylor, John Geraghty, Jonathan DeHart, Alan Weinberg, and Andrew Mallamo are in blue. The second string, Brendan Buso, Jack Van Norden, Fasil Girmay, Chris Skallerup, and Jason Chun, switch to gold.

Chris and the other second stringers stood at the side of the court twisting their reversible practice jerseys to the gold side and pulling them over their heads.

"Man, they've got a slaughter team again," Jason muttered.

"Yeah, I can't believe Coach is playing first string against the second string *again*," Chris said. "They're gonna kill us."

"Come on, guys," Brendan said bravely. "We can beat them."

"Something the matter, gold team?" Coach Anderson asked, holding the ball in one hand and his whistle in the other.

"The teams just don't seem fair, Coach," Jason said.

The coach studied the teams more closely. "You're right. Now what can we do to make them fair?"

John Geraghty spoke up: "How about we'll give them a three-basket lead?"

"Heck, we'll give them four baskets," said Dontae, the Eagles high-scoring star forward.

What a showoff, thought Chris.

"All right, 4–0. Gold's ahead," Coach Anderson announced, snapping a quick bounce pass to Jason. "Gold ball. Game to ten baskets. Losing team runs laps around the gym."

The Eagles, especially the second stringers, groaned.

The scrimmage went much as the second stringers had expected. The Eagles first team used their speed and better skills to cut away quickly at the second string's four-basket lead.

14

Chris tried to cover Dontae Taylor. The game was moving fast and the score was 5–3. John Geraghty passed to Dontae on the right wing. After Dontae caught the ball, he raised the ball as if he were about to shoot. Chris leaped into the air hoping to block the shot, but Dontae brought the ball down and dribbled by Chris for an easy basket.

"5–4. Gold lead!" Coach Anderson shouted. "Don't leave your feet on defense, Chris. Wait until he jumps before you jump."

"Yeah, Skallerup," Dontae teased as they ran downcourt. "No way you're gonna stop me by leaving your feet."

Still, the second string did not quit. They clung to their narrow lead as Brendan Buso and Fasil Girmay swished long jump shots and Chris scored on a driving layup.

But Chris just could not stop Dontae. He drove by Chris and dished a perfect bounce pass to Alan, who hooked in the tying basket.

"8–8," Coach Anderson called. "You've gotta stay low on defense, Chris. Keep moving your feet."

Jason missed a shot for the second string and John Geraghty snapped down the rebound.

"Johnny!" Dontae yelled as he sprinted downcourt to the blue team's basket. Chris tried to race back with Dontae but it was too late. Johnny's long pass hit Dontae in stride and the Eagles star forward dropped in the go-ahead basket. 9–8.

The second string moved the ball around looking for a good shot. But Brendan's shot to tie the game rolled around the rim and slipped off. Dontae swooped in, got the ball, dribbled by Chris, and passed to Jonathan standing deep in the corner. Chris's shoulders and spirits sank as Jonathan's shot swished through the net. The first string had won again, 10–8.

"All right, gold team!" Coach Anderson shouted. "Give me five laps around the gym."

After the laps, Chris stood bent over at the waist, gasping for breath.

Phweeet!

"Let's pair up for the 90-second drill," Coach Anderson called, pointing to the baskets around the gym. "You know the drill: one player shoots; one player rebounds for the shooter. The shooter has to keep moving to a new spot after each shot. See how many baskets you can get in 90 seconds. Rebounders, keep track of the baskets."

Chris rebounded for Jason in the first round. Chris snapped sharp passes to his friend as Jason sent jump shot after jump shot up to the hoop.

Phweeet!

Coach Anderson's whistle stopped the action. He pointed at each pair of players and asked,

"How many did you get?"

"10...15...9...12...16," the answers came back from around the gym. The coach marked the answers down on a chart posted on the wall.

"Okay, next shooters," he called.

Chris stood fifteen feet away from the basket, spun the ball in his hands, and waited for the coach to sound his whistle to signal the start of the drill.

Phweeet!

Chris's first shot bounced off the rim. Jason scrambled after the rebound. Chris kept shooting and Jason kept count as Coach Anderson shouted instructions to the shooters.

"Keep your legs moving!"

"Concentrate on the rim!"

"Face the basket!"

"Follow through with your wrist."

Finally, the coach looked at his watch and counted down the final seconds.

"Five...four...three...two..."

Chris launched a long jump shot just as Coach Anderson's whistle blew.

Swish!

"Count it!" Coach Anderson said as he pointed to Jason and asked, "How many did he get?"

"Eight."

"Not bad." The coach collected more numbers from around the gym, marked them on the chart,

Chris's first shot bounced off the rim.

and then blew his whistle. "Good practice," he said. "Hit the showers."

The team started toward the double doors at the end of the gym. "Remember, we've got a game at two o'clock on Saturday," the coach called. "Be ready to play. The Rosemont Rockets are tough."

Chris and Jason stood near the doors studying the chart on the wall.

90-SECOND DRILL

PLAYER	12/17	12/22	1/5	1/7	1/12	1/14	1/20	
Buso, Brendan	11	12	14	12	11			
Chun, Jason	7	9	11	9	12			
DeHart, Jonathan	13	13	12	14	12			
Geraghty, John	15	12	15	14	16			
Girmay, Fasil	7	10	10	11	8			
Mallamo, Andrew	10	12	9	13	14			
Skallerup, Chris	8	7	10	9	8			
Taylor, Dontae	14	16	15	14	20			
Van Norden, Jack	11	12	7	13	9			
Weinberg, Alan	10	9	11	11	14			

"Man," Chris said, shaking his head at the columns of numbers. "I'm about the worst shooter on the team."

"Eight is not so bad," Jason said. "I'm not much better."

"You got twelve, that's pretty good." Chris looked at the numbers again. "Wow! Look at Dontae," he said, pointing at the paper. "He got twenty today!"

Chris looked at the floor and shook his head sadly. "I couldn't get twenty if they let me shoot for 90 *minutes.*"

"Stop worrying about your shooting," Jason said. "It'll get better."

"I sure hope so," Chris answered. "Or I'll be stuck at the end of the bench forever."

"What's so bad about that?" Jason protested.

"What do you mean?" Chris asked.

"Hey, at least you'll be with me," Jason answered. The two friends laughed and headed through the doors to the showers.

FOUR

"Come on, Dontae!" Coach Anderson shouted from the bench. "Let's play some defense. Stay low and move your feet."

The Eagles, sitting beside their coach, chimed in with more cheers.

"Let's go, Eagles!"

"Hands up, guys!"

"Back on D! Back on D!"

Chris and Jason fidgeted at the end of the hardwood bench. Jason rubbed his hands across his bare arms and whispered to Chris, "Man, I'm freezing. Don't they heat this gym on weekends?"

"We'd be a lot warmer if Coach would put us in," Chris answered. Chris leaned forward and looked down the bench to Coach Anderson. The coach shook his head in frustration as a Rosemont Rocket guard slipped by the Eagles defense and scored on a layup.

"Come on, pick him up. Let's play some defense."

Chris looked up at the scoreboard.

A minute to go in the third quarter, down by eight, Chris thought.

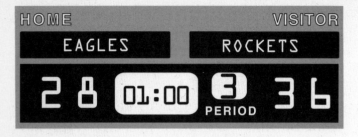

Just then Jason whispered what Chris was secretly thinking. "I wish Rosemont would score a few more baskets so Coach would put us in the game."

"Hey," Chris whispered back. "We're not supposed to root against our own team."

"I just want to play," Jason said, as he reached past Chris and poured himself water from the bucket at the end of the Eagles bench.

"You'd better not drink too much water," Chris warned, "or you'll be in the bathroom before you get in the game."

"We're not gonna get in this game," Jason said, gulping his water.

"Sure we will," Chris said with a voice full of determination but not much hope.

Jason shook his head, smiled, then whispered to Chris, "I wonder if we could bring popcorn so we could sit back and watch the game in style."

"Hey," Chris whispered back. "We're not supposed
to root against our team."

On the court, the Eagles passed the ball around, looking for the last shot before the end of the third quarter. Glancing at the clock, Chris and the rest of the bench-warming Eagles began a countdown to tell their teammates on the floor that time was running out. "Ten...nine...eight..."

Jonathan DeHart passed the ball to John Geraghty deep in the corner and John tossed up a three-point prayer.

Swish.

The Eagle bench was on its feet cheering. But Chris was thinking, *Oh, great, now I'll never get in the game.*

At the break, the Eagles starting lineup sat on the bench while Coach Anderson knelt on one knee and gave his instructions for the final quarter. Chris and the other second stringers stood in back of the coach.

"Okay guys, let's keep working the ball around for good shots," the coach said. "Great shot at the end, John. That kept us in it. But we've got to play better defense. Stay low in good defensive position, just like in practice. And don't give them any easy shots!"

Chris and Jason reached to put their hands in a circle with their other teammates.

"Let's get it done," Coach Anderson shouted.

Chris and Jason took their familiar seats at the

24

end of the Eagles bench. Jason leaned over to Chris and whispered, "I was just wondering, if we don't get in, do we have to take a shower after the game?"

"We'll get in," Chris said.

Jason looked down the bench to Coach Anderson and then back at Chris and silently mouthed the words *Go Rockets.*

As if granting Jason's wish, the Rockets raced out to a big lead. The Eagles defense gave up easy shot after easy shot to the fired-up Rockets. Jason and Chris quickly glanced at each other. "Hey, maybe we are gonna get in after all," Jason whispered.

Chris nodded and said, "Looks like it."

"Think we should have rooted against our own team?" Jason asked, suddenly sounding guilty.

Chris shrugged his shoulders and looked up at the scoreboard.

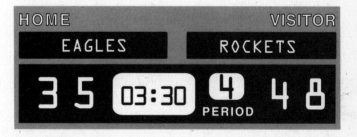

Within seconds the Rockets made another basket. Coach Anderson threw up his hands and threw down his towel.

"Chris, Jason, go in for Dontae and Jonathan!" he called down the bench.

In a flash, Chris and Jason were at the scorer's table. "Skallerup and Chun, in for Taylor and DeHart," Chris said to the scorer and then turned to face the court and knelt on one knee in front of the scorer's table.

"Garbage time," Jason whispered as the two teammates waited anxiously for the next time-out. The buzzer blared and Chris looked at the clock as he walked on to the floor. *Three minutes and three seconds to show the coach I can really play,* he thought.

The time went by in a blur. Fasil Girmay passed to Chris for a wide-open fifteen-foot jump shot. The ball felt good as it left Chris's hand, but it caught the rim and bounced back into Jason's outstretched hands. Jason dipped and pushed the ball back up toward the basket. It was good! But the glory didn't last long. The Rockets took possession of the ball and swiftly moved it downcourt for another lightning-quick two points. The Eagles scored again—a three-pointer by Jack Van Norden—but the Rockets answered that basket with two more of their own. It was coming down to the final seconds of the game. Chris had the ball near the basket and took a shot. It fell short as the buzzer sounded long and loud. The Rockets had won: 54 to 40.

After shaking the Rockets hands, Chris and Jason stood at the side of the court. "I barely got warmed up," Chris said, shaking his head and remembering his two missed shots.

"Hey, I got a basket," Jason blurted out happily. "And look at us," he said, shaking his hair. "We're sweating like crazy. We've got to take showers now!" The two friends laughed and headed for the locker room. Chris saw his mother and father on the way.

"Good game, Chris," his mother said kindly.

"Too bad you didn't get to play more," his dad said.

Chris shrugged. "I've got to make my shots if I want to play more. I missed two," he said, looking down at his feet.

"Too bad you guys lost," someone called out. Chris looked up again. Greta was standing in the bleachers. "Rosemont has a really good team," she added.

"When does your team play Rosemont?" Chris asked Greta.

Before Greta could speak, her teammate and friend Sharon Hanley answered for her, "Tuesday afternoon, after your practice."

"Yeah, you guys should stick around and watch," Greta said.

"I hope you have better luck," Chris said.

"We'll beat them," Greta said confidently. "And it won't be luck."

FIVE

Chris and Jason sat on the last row of the bleachers, leaning back against the cold tile of the gymnasium wall. Chris ran his fingers through his hair, which was still slicked back from his post-practice shower.

On the floor below, the girls' teams went through their warm-up drills. The Eagle girls passed the ball smartly around the floor as they flashed to the basket for layup after layup.

"What's their record?" Jason asked.

"I think they're 3–0," Chris answered.

"I bet nobody can cover Gretzky," Jason said. "She must be scoring fifty points a game."

"No, more like twenty-five."

Chris leaned forward, resting his elbows on his knees and his chin in his hands. He watched Greta glide around the court in her crisp blue uniform with a gold 45 on her back, white wristbands, white socks, and white high-tops. Her blond hair was pulled back and clipped tight and her feet seemed to barely touch the floor.

"Do they have anybody else who's any good?" Jason asked.

Chris pointed his finger. "Sharon Hanley is supposed to be pretty good."

"She's good at everything," Jason said.

"And Erin Geraghty, John's older sister, is tall," Chris continued, "so she gets a lot of rebounds. The Geraghtys are a basketball family. Even their kid sister Elizabeth plays. She's only eight years old but she can throw them in the basket at Green Street."

The Eagle girls formed a semicircle around the basket to practice their jump shots.

Chris narrowed his eyes and studied Greta closely. He silently counted how many straight shots Greta sent through the net.

Seven...eight...nine...ten...eleven...

The buzzer at the scorer's table blasted through the gym to signal the beginning of the game. Greta flung a final shot high into the air. She turned to walk to the bench, never bothering to watch the ball splash through the net.

Chris leaned back and shook his head in disbelief. "She's unbelievable," he blurted out. "She never misses."

"What are you talking about?" Jason asked.

"Gretzky," Chris answered. "She just hit twelve shots in a row!"

"So what," Jason said, making a face and sounding unimpressed. "She makes twelve in a row all the time down at Green Street."

"Yeah, but...but..." Chris stammered, at a loss for words. "She's great."

"Hey, tell me something I don't know." Jason laughed.

The game between the Eagles and the Rockets was neck and neck. The Rosemont Rockets coach waved her arms and warned her team to cover Greta.

"Watch out for 45!" she shouted. "Get on her, now. She's trouble!"

But neither the Rockets coach nor the Rockets players could stop Greta. She moved easily around the Rockets trying to cover her. She scored on long jump shots and zipped passes to wide-open team-mates. Every time one of Greta's shots fell through the net, a woman sitting alone in the bleachers would spring up and shout, "All right, Greta! Good shot. Good shot."

Chris looked over to Jason. "Is that Gretzky's mom?" he asked. "She can really yell."

Jason nodded. "Yeah, I guess Gretzky's the shooter in the family and her mother is the shouter."

During halftime, Chris looked up at the score-board. "Gretzky's doing great," he said. "But it's still pretty close. 22–18."

But in the first few minutes of the second half, Greta took over the game. First she darted out to steal a careless Rocket pass and dribbled the length of the

Just outside the three-point arc she suddenly stopped and sent a perfect high jump shot sailing to the basket.

court for an easy basket. Then she whirled around, stole the inbound pass, and hit a quick jumper.

The Rockets dribbled downcourt and missed a long shot. Greta snapped down the rebound, spun around, and dribbled back down the court. Just outside the three-point arc she suddenly stopped and sent a perfect high jump shot sailing to the basket.

Swish!

"Time-out. Time-out," the Rockets coach called, her hands forming a frustrated *T*.

Chris and Jason stood and exchanged high fives in the bleachers. Chris glanced at the scoreboard. Suddenly the Eagles were ahead by eleven, 29–18, and the game was as good as over.

The Eagle girls danced onto the floor and swarmed around Greta. In the stands, Greta's mother was dancing too. "That's my girl!" she yelled. "That's my girl."

Chris settled back into his seat, staring at Greta as the crowd's cheers echoed off the gym walls and fell like confetti all around her.

"Man," Jason said, still standing and clapping his hands in admiration, "that girl can shoot."

"Yeah," Chris said quietly. His eyes followed Greta as she walked back onto the court after time-out.

What I wouldn't give, Chris thought, *to be able to shoot like that.*

SIX

On Saturday morning, Chris stood at the top of the hill overlooking Green Street Park. Near one of the basketball hoops a single figure, dressed in a bright red sweatshirt and red sweatpants, was moving the snow off the court. The sound of the shovel scraping across the tarmac cut the icy quiet.

Chris carefully edged his way down the hill. His sneakers slipped and slid on the fresh snow. At the bottom of the hill, a big, black Labrador retriever bounded toward him.

"Hey, Mingo," Chris greeted the dog, giving him a friendly rub behind his ears.

"Hey, Gretzky!" Chris shouted across the cold and snow. Greta turned abruptly, surprised that she wasn't alone.

"Hey, Chris," she said. "What are you doing here? I thought I'd be the only person crazy enough to come here today."

Chris blew hot breath on his cold hands and squinted into the bright winter sky.

"It's not so bad," he said as he walked across the court. Greta went back to piling the snow off to the side.

"Did you bring a broom or anything?" she asked.

Chris shook his head. "Uh, no. But maybe we can take turns shoveling."

"That's okay. This snow is light. It'll only take another minute. Then the sun will dry off the court."

Chris kept blowing on his hands and shifting his weight from one foot to the other. "I saw your game against the Rockets," he said. "You were great. How many points did you score?"

"I don't really keep track."

"I'll bet you must have had thirty points. Easy."

"Something like that." Greta shrugged.

With one half of the court clear, Greta stuck her shovel into a new pile of snow and picked up her basketball. As she dribbled against the still-wet tarmac, the ball made a series of noisy splats. Greta dribbled past the foul line, spun to her left, and shot an off-balance jump shot.

Swish!

Chris grabbed the rebound. "How do you shoot like that?" he blurted out as he tossed the ball back to Greta.

"What do you mean?" Greta asked as she caught the ball and shot again.

Another *swish*.

"Like that," Chris said, pointing to the basket. "How do you shoot like that? I watched you before the Rockets game. You must have hit twelve in a row."

"I don't know," Greta answered, sounding a bit confused. "I practice a lot, I guess." She took another shot. The ball touched off the backboard and dropped through the net.

"I practice a lot, too. And all my shots bounce off the rim," Chris said.

"Not all of them," Greta corrected.

"Well, most of them do," Chris said as he watched another shot by Greta drop in. "A lot more of mine bounce off the rim than yours. That's for sure."

Finally, one of Greta's shots did bounce off the rim and Chris grabbed the rebound.

"Will you teach me to shoot like you?" he asked, holding the ball in two hands and looking straight at Greta. Greta's face curled up as if Chris had asked her something really weird. And Chris suddenly felt a little dumb for asking.

"You want me to teach you how to shoot?" Greta asked.

"Well, like, um, just give me some tips or something," Chris said, shrugging his shoulders. "I just figured if I could shoot better, Coach Anderson would give me some more playing time. I mean, come on, Greta, you're the best shooter I know."

As Chris waited for Greta's reply, a cold gust swept across the park and sent a stinging spray of snow onto Chris's cheeks. He shut his eyes tight and wiped the snow away. When he opened his eyes again he saw Greta staring at him, deep in thought.

"Let's see you take a shot," she said finally, motioning toward the basket.

Chris took a jump shot. The ball hit the rim, wobbled a little, and slipped through the net.

"Take another," Greta said.

His second shot bounced off the rim and fell to the wet ground.

Splat!

"You've got your elbow too far out," Greta said.

"What?"

"You've got to keep your elbow closer to your body," Greta repeated. "Give me the ball. I'll show you."

Chris brought the ball to Greta and stood beside her as she showed him how to shoot. "You've got to hold the ball on your fingers, not back on your palm." Greta balanced the ball gently on her fingertips. "Keep your elbow in, under the ball," she continued, tucking her elbow in close to her body. "Square your shoulders so you're facing the basket and get a strong push off with your legs." Greta sent the ball spinning to the basket.

Swish!

"So you'll help me?" Chris asked, excitedly.

"Yeah, I guess so." Greta smiled. "But only when there aren't enough kids around for a real game. I'd rather play ball than teach it."

"Hey, no problem," Chris agreed. "Anytime you've got enough for a game, go for it."

Chris dribbled back to the spot next to Greta, suddenly certain that his dream of Coach Anderson giving him more playing time was closer than ever before. He looked at Greta and repeated her instructions. "Ball on the fingers, elbows in, face the basket, push off with the legs." Chris's shot flew to the basket, bounced off the rim, and fell once again to the ground.

Splat!

SEVEN

A couple of weeks later, Chris, Greta, and Jason were back at Green Street Park.

"Go!" Jason shouted from the side of the court as he pushed a button on his wristwatch. Chris's first jump shot rattled around the rim and fell in.

"One!" Greta shouted. She grabbed the rebound and passed the ball to Chris. The next shot teetered on the rim but didn't go in.

"Keep your elbow in. Follow through with your wrist," Greta called.

Chris concentrated on keeping his elbow in and began to make some shots.

"That's it," said Greta. "Keep your legs moving. Push off."

But Chris's streak didn't last. The next few shots clanged against the rim.

"Thirty seconds," Jason called as he stared at his watch. Chris swished a long shot from the corner.

"That's eight!" Greta yelled. "Keep your eye on the rim. Don't watch the ball."

Swish!

"Nine. You've got twenty seconds."

Chris caught the ball and took a quick shot. As the ball left his hands, he could tell it was going in.

"Ten. Ten more seconds left."

Another quick shot fell short.

Greta hustled over, grabbed the ball, and fired a bullet pass to Chris, who had his hands wide open for it. Jason quickly looked at his watch and counted down.

"Three...two..."

Chris let go of the shot right at the count of "one." It sailed straight through the net.

"It's good!" yelled Jason.

"How many did I get?" Chris asked Greta as he tried to catch his breath.

"Eleven," Greta answered.

"Hey, that's not bad," said Jason.

"It's not great," Greta sniffed.

"Does the girls' team ever do 90-second drills, Gretzky?" Chris asked, still huffing and puffing.

"Sometimes," Greta said as she spun in for a twisting left-handed layup.

"What's the most shots you've ever gotten?" Chris asked, although he wasn't sure he wanted to know the answer.

"Twenty-eight."

"Huh?" Chris asked, his mouth hanging wide open.

"Twenty-eight."

"Tha—that's better than Dontae," he sputtered.

"I'm a better shooter than Dontae," she said without hesitation.

"Man, twenty-eight," Chris repeated, still stunned.

"Hey, you're getting better," Jason said to him.

"Yeah," Greta agreed. "Your shot is looking better. Your elbow is in, you're facing the basket and—"

"And I still stink at shooting," Chris said before Greta could finish the sentence.

Greta and Jason were silent. Chris stretched his arms out as if he were looking for help. "Come on, guys," he pleaded. "I thought you were my buddies. You should be saying, 'You don't stink at shooting, Chris. No way you stink at shooting.'"

"Well, you don't stink as bad as you used to," Jason offered.

Chris laughed, mostly at himself. "Thanks a lot, buddy."

"How many practices have we had?" Chris asked Greta finally.

"A bunch," she said, bouncing the ball on the damp tarmac. A light snow was starting to fall.

"Maybe I'll never be a good shooter no matter how much I practice," Chris said sadly.

"Hey, maybe Gretzky's just a bad teacher," Jason teased.

Greta didn't laugh.

"I'm kidding," Jason said.

The snow was starting to stick and the sky had darkened. "I'd better get going," Jason said, and he started up the hill. "I've got lots of homework."

Mingo romped up to Greta, who bent over and rubbed noses with him. The dog licked Greta's face. "Okay, Mingo. We'll get going," she laughed. "Just let me hit my last shot."

Chris searched his pockets. "Oh no," he said. "I forgot my house key. I don't know if I'll be able to get in."

"Why don't you come to my house?" Greta suggested as she and Mingo started up the hill. "You can call your house to see if anyone's home."

The two friends and Mingo walked briskly through the lightly falling snow.

"Hey, Gretzky, where do you live, anyway?" Chris asked as they walked. "I've never been to your house. I guess I figured you just lived at Green Street Park."

"You're right. I live at Green Street, but I sleep at the corner of Second and Luzerne."

"In the little house with the blue door?" Chris asked.

Greta nodded. "Yeah, but it's plenty big enough for my mom and me." She paused and added, "And Mingo."

"What about your dad?" Chris asked, but

then felt sorry for asking.

"He lives in California," Greta said matter-of-factly. "My mom and dad got divorced when I was real little. So it's just my mom and me. My mom's pretty cool. Come on, let's walk a little faster."

Within minutes, Chris, Greta, and Mingo were at Greta's door. As they stepped into the front hall, Mingo shook himself dry. Chris ran his hand through his snow-wet hair and looked at his sneakers.

"Should I take my shoes off?" Chris asked.

"What for?" Greta asked.

"They're kinda wet and dirty."

"That's okay." Greta stepped into the living room. "Mimi," she called.

"Who's Mimi?" Chris asked

"My mom. It's her real name. When I was little I got it confused with 'mommy,' and it just sort of stuck."

"I'm in my office, Greta," her mom called from the back of the house.

Chris and Greta walked through the dining room, past a plastic tub of dirty laundry on a chair, through the kitchen with breakfast dishes still on the table, and into an office where Greta's mom sat among stacks of books, papers, and forgotten cups of coffee. She was looking at a computer screen as she typed away on the keyboard propped on her lap.

"Hey, Mimi," Greta said breezily. "We have company."

Mimi turned to her daughter and asked, "Who?"

Chris walked through the doorway. "This is Chris Skallerup," Greta said. "You know. I'm showing him how to shoot better."

Chris put out his hand and said, "It's nice to meet you, Mrs. Pemberton."

"Um, my mom's last name is different from mine. It's Remage," Greta said.

Chris blushed. But Greta's mom smiled and said, "Just call me Mimi, Chris. All the kids do. Tell me, how are the lessons going?"

"Okay, I guess," said Chris. "But I still can't shoot like Greta."

"You ought to talk to my mom," Greta said proudly. "She was a big basketball star when she was in high school."

"Really?" Chris said, suddenly interested. "How many points did you score a game?"

Mimi Remage tilted back her head and laughed. "I never scored," she said.

EIGHT

"You never scored?!" Chris repeated. "How could you be a basketball star if you never scored?"

Mimi laughed again. "Heck, I never even took a shot," she said.

A questioning look crossed Chris's face. "Yeah, but...but..." he stammered.

"Are you kids thirsty?" Mimi asked. Chris and Greta nodded. Her mom shut down the computer. "Come on, let's go into the kitchen and get you two something to drink while I explain old-time girls' basketball to Chris."

Chris and Greta sat at the kitchen table while Mimi squatted like a baseball catcher in front of the opened refrigerator. She moved her head from side to side, searching the crowded bottom shelf. Finally she reached in and pulled out two green bottles. "How about some ginger ale?"

"Sure," Chris said.

Mimi twisted off the caps and placed the bottles on the table. "Do you mind drinking out of the bottle? We don't have any clean glasses."

Chris took a long swig of ginger ale. He put his hand over his mouth to smother a small burp as Greta's mom started to talk.

"You see, I was brought up in a small town in Iowa. And up until a few years ago, girls played six-on-six basketball."

"You mean there were six kids on each team? I thought basketball was always five-on-five," Chris said. "How did you play?"

"Let me show you," Mimi said as she sat down at the table and pushed papers and dishes off to the side. Then she turned over a cup and a rush of coins spilled out and clattered across the table. She picked through the coins on the table. "Let's say the pennies are one team," she said, "and the quarters are the other team."

"The salt and pepper shakers can be the baskets," Greta suggested, moving them into position.

Chris leaned across the table and listened intently as he sipped his ginger ale *slowly* so he wouldn't burp.

"You see, each team had six players," Mimi continued, moving the coins about the table.

"Six players," Chris exclaimed. "Didn't it get awfully crowded?"

"Not really, because no one played the whole court," Mimi explained.

"Let me show you," Mimi said as she sat down at the table
and pushed papers and dishes off to the side.

"How did they play, then?" Chris asked.

"We could each only play on half of the court. Three of our players played offense all the time on one half of the court and the other three players played defense on the other half."

"You mean you couldn't ever go over the center-court line?"

"That's right." Mimi smiled, remembering. "I used to race up to the half-court line and stop as if it was the edge of a cliff."

"Seems kinda stupid," Chris said, leaning back from the table. "Why didn't they let all the girls go full-court like the boys?"

Mimi shrugged. "I don't know. I guess they thought girls were too weak and delicate to play full-court."

"That's *really* stupid," Chris said. "Gretzky can outrun most of the boys at school."

Greta stood up and flexed the muscle on her right arm and then laughed.

Mimi smiled and said quietly, "It was a long time ago. Things were different then."

Chris nodded. "So I guess you just played defense for your high school team."

"*Just* played defense!" Greta protested. "She was the best. Hey, Mimi, why don't I get the scrapbook to show Chris?"

"Oh, he doesn't want to see those old newspaper

47

clippings," her mom said, waving away the suggestion with her hand.

"Sure I do," Chris said excitedly.

Greta bolted from the room. In a flash, she returned with a red leather three-ring binder. Greta laid the book out on the kitchen table, flipping through the neatly matted pages.

"Here's a good one," she said, pointing to an old newspaper article.

"Wow, that's cool," Chris said. "Did your team win the state championship?"

Mimi shook her head. "No, we lost in the quarterfinals. A girl named Mary Ann Szwed threw in a jumper at the buzzer," she recalled in a voice that made it seem as if she were back at the game seeing the buzzer-basket all over again.

HIGH SCHOOLS

Adel defeats Ankeny 82-64; qualifies for tourney

FROM STAFF REPORTS

The spirited play of defender Mimi Remage sparked Adel to an easy 82-64 win over Ankeny and a place in the state tournament. Nancy Tolar led Adel with 51 points, and Remage held Ankeny's high-scoring forward Erin McClure to only 25 points, almost 20 points below her season average.

The Adel Class AAAA team, ranked No. 1 in the state, advances to the state semifinals which begin next Saturday.

—*Michael Forsythe*

MORE BASKETBALL

Top-ranked Class AA/A Roswell beat McNair in a 78-74 squeaker in the girls Area 3 championship game. In the boys final, Riverwood (11-3-3) edged out No. 7 Collier Hills

led (
80-7
Jean
49 p
held
forw
22 |
belo

Gler
84 ir
over
edge
Aca
goal
Dav

led (
80-7
Jean
49 p
held
forw
22 |
belo

Gler
84 ir
over
edge
Aca
goal
Dav

48

"Hey, Chris, weren't you going to call your house?" Greta asked suddenly.

"Oh yeah," Chris said, still turning the pages of the old scrapbook.

"The phone's over there," Mimi said, pointing to it on the kitchen wall beside a sign that said: "Bless this mess."

But Chris barely heard her. He was lost in the old newspaper stories—and in the beginning of a new idea.

NINE

On Saturday morning, Chris stood once again at Greta's door. A brisk wind swirled around him as he rang the bell. The door swung open, and Greta stood inside dressed in her sweatshirt, sweatpants, and high-top sneakers. Her hair was pulled back.

"I figured it was you," she said brightly. "You ready for another shooting lesson?"

Greta did not wait for Chris to answer but waved him inside. "Come on in," she said. "It looks kind of windy. Might be a tough day for shooting."

"Wind never seems to bother you," Chris said.

"Yeah, let me get my hat and we'll get going." Greta started to rummage through a wicker basket overflowing with scarves, gloves, hats, and boots. Mingo bounded past Chris, pushed open the door, and ran out with his nose high in the air, sniffing the new day.

"You know, Gretzky," Chris started. "I...I...was kind of thinking about something."

"Here it is," Greta said as she pulled out a wool

cap and put it on. "Now what were you saying?"

"Well, I was just saying that I was just thinking..." Chris stopped in midsentence and then blurted out, "Is your mom around?"

"Sure," Greta said, a bit confused. "What do you want her for?"

Chris finally told Greta what he had been thinking about ever since he had looked through her mother's scrapbook a few days before. "I was kind of thinking that maybe she could teach me how to play defense," Chris said. "You know, like she played in high school."

"You don't want to practice your jump shot anymore?" Greta asked.

"No, it's not that. I'll keep practicing my jump shot," Chris assured her. "But I figure if I get good at defense, the coach might give me more playing time in the games. You know how coaches are always saying how important defense is."

"Yeah," Greta laughed. "But they always play the kids who can score."

Chris asked his question again with his eyes. Greta looked at Chris for a long moment, just as she had when Chris had asked her to teach him to shoot.

"Mimi," she called over her shoulder.

Mimi came walking into the front entrance in slippers and sweats with a steaming cup of coffee in her hand. "Hi, Chris. You kids going down to

51

the park this morning?"

"Well, yeah," said Greta. "But Chris wants you to come along and teach him how to play defense."

Mimi laughed. "What?" she asked, almost spilling her coffee.

Chris turned a little red but he spoke up. "Yeah, Mrs. Pember—I mean, Mimi. I figure I'll never be a great shooter like Gretzky. But I think I could get really good at defense—with a little help."

Mimi took a long gulp of coffee. "Well, sure. I'd love to show you how to play defense," she said, sounding pleased. She glanced at her daughter. "*Greta* won't let me teach her anything," she teased.

"Mom!" Greta protested.

"Just kidding," her mom said. "Let me get my sneakers and we'll get going." Within minutes, the three were standing on the cold tarmac at Green Street Park. Mingo was roaming about, searching for old tennis balls. The wind swept across the snow-covered baseball diamond and empty tennis courts.

"Let's see if I remember this stuff," Mimi chuckled as she took her defensive stance in front of Chris and Greta. She called out her instructions as she began to move around the court and remembered: "Keep your feet about shoulder-width apart. And keep one foot slightly behind the other."

Chris stood in his stance a few feet away. Mimi eyed him up and down. "Flex your knees more," she demanded. "And get your tushy down."

"Mom!" Greta shouted.

"What?!"

"Don't talk about tushies!" Greta raised her voice and rolled her eyes.

"Okay, okay," her mom said. "Chris, get your bottom down!"

"I knew what you meant," Chris said.

"Good!" she said. "Now Greta, you try to dribble by Chris. Nothing fancy, just try to get by him." Greta dribbled smoothly to the right. After a few quick steps, Chris came out of his stance and ran beside her.

"No, no," Mimi said firmly. "You've got to stay in your defensive stance and move your feet from side to side. Let me show you."

Mimi got into her stance across from Greta. "Concentrate on the player's hips, not the ball," she instructed. Then she said, "Go ahead, Greta, try to get by me."

This time, Greta dribbled to the left. Staying low, Mimi moved swiftly to block Greta's path to the basket. Greta stopped her dribble and held the ball and tried to shoot. Her mother moved closer to her and waved her arms.

"When a player stops and picks up her dribble, really go after her," she said, "because you know she can't stop dribbling and then start again. Once you

Mimi got into her stance across from Greta. "Concentrate on the player's hips, not the ball," she instructed.

stop her she's got to pass or shoot."

"Okay, Mimi," Greta said, moving the ball away. "Take it easy."

"Take it easy?!" Mimi repeated, pretending to be shocked. "You *never* take it easy on defense."

She clapped her hands and looked straight at Chris. "All right, let's get to work on you."

For the next hour, the three worked on Chris's defense. Mimi gave instructions and encouragement as Chris tried to cover Greta.

"Move your feet, Chris."

"Bend your knees."

"Good hustle. That's it."

"Get that tushy—I mean bottom—down."

At the end of the workout, Chris plopped down on the hard tarmac. His deep, quick breaths sent fast, white puffs into the cold air.

"Man, defense is hard work," he said, still breathing hard.

"Nothing but hard work," Mimi agreed. "That's another thing," she said. "You've gotta get into really good shape. You can't get tired on defense. You've gotta make the other guy get tired."

"Maybe Chris could come on our morning runs with us," Greta suggested. "That would get him in shape." Greta turned to Chris. "You want to?" she asked.

Chris straightened up and took another gulp of

air. "Sure," he said as pushed off the ground and stood up, rising to the challenge.

Mimi glanced at her watch. "I'd better get going," she said.

"Remember, Mimi," Greta said as she passed her mother the ball, "you always have to sink your last shot."

Standing about fifteen feet from the basket, Mimi bent at the knees and sent an awkward one-hand push shot at the hoop. The ball smacked off the backboard and rim and bounced away. Mingo saw it go and went chasing after it.

Mimi laughed. "I never could shoot that thing," she said.

TEN

The sunrise stretched a ribbon of red across the horizon. Beneath the streetlights, Chris, Greta, and Mimi jogged side by side through the quiet early morning darkness. The crunch of sand and old snow under their feet and the rhythm of their steady breathing were the only sounds. Mingo ran alongside, tied to the group by the long leash in Mimi's hand.

They passed Greta's house, and Chris knew that the daily morning run was half over.

One more lap to go, he thought. As he jogged steadily through the still morning air, Chris remembered how tired he had felt on his first run just two weeks before when the group had passed the halfway mark. Chris could feel himself getting stronger day by day. His arms and legs moved in a fluid, almost effortless fashion. His feet barely touched the ground.

"How are you doing?" Mimi asked, glancing at Chris.

"Fine. Great," Chris answered confidently.

"Only a couple of weeks of running and you're getting in pretty good shape," Mimi observed.

"Almost as good as Gretzky." Chris smiled.

"Almost," Greta answered with a big grin.

"How's basketball going?" Mimi asked, tugging a bit at Mingo's leash.

"Not so good," Chris answered, his eyes staring off down the street where a man driving a slow-moving van was throwing newspapers onto lawns. "I'm still stuck on the end of the bench with Jason and the water jug. I'm playing better in practice, but Coach Anderson doesn't seem to notice."

"It takes time. He'll notice."

"How's your shooting?" Greta asked.

"Better. I got fourteen baskets last practice in the 90-second drill. That's the best score I've ever gotten," Chris said. "It's almost as good as your record of twenty-eight," he added kiddingly.

"Almost," Greta answered.

"I just hope I get a chance to play against the Wood Acres Wildcats." Chris kept talking, surprised that he still had breath to talk. "They've got Tim Cooney, he's a big scorer. Maybe the coach will let me try to stop him."

"When do you play them?" Greta asked.

"Next week," Chris said. "So I've only got one more practice to show the coach what I can do." The group continued running through the streets of the waking town. Lights were going on inside the houses.

"When do you play the Wildcats?" Chris asked Greta.

"Couple of days."

Chris nodded. "They've got Lily Harris, don't they? She's supposed to be great."

"I've played her. She's not so hot," Greta said, unimpressed.

"She scores about twenty points a game," Chris argued.

"How good can she be?" Greta sniffed. "She paints her nails bright pink."

"What do her fingernails have to do with how good she is?" Mimi asked.

"You know what I mean," Greta answered.

"You really shouldn't make fun of the other players like that," Mimi scolded.

"Okay," Greta sighed as if she had heard this a million times. "I'll try not to make fun of other players if you try not yell so much in the stands during the game."

"All right. I'll try," Mimi said.

The early morning sun began to peek over the trees. In the dim sunlight Chris could see Greta's house down at the end of a long block.

I feel great, he thought. *I hardly feel like I've been running.* Chris glanced quickly to his left at Greta.

59

"I'll race you to your house, Gretzky!" he shouted over his shoulder as he sprinted away.

"Hey, no fair!" Greta yelled as she lurched forward and started to pick up speed. "You got a head start."

"Be careful, you two," her mother warned. "It's still pretty dark. Don't trip."

But Chris and Greta were off and racing, flying across the cold, flat, empty street. Chris's surprise start gave him the early lead. He was running as fast as he could with his legs churning and his arms pumping. His eyes were fixed on Greta's house off in the distance.

Chris was trying desperately to hold on to his lead but he could sense Greta over his left shoulder slowly gaining on him. In no time she was running alongside him. Chris sneaked a look to his left and then focused straight ahead. *About one hundred yards to go*, he thought.

The two friends ran stride for stride, their footfalls slapping down on the cold tarmac in unison. Again Chris glanced over at Greta. She looked calm and focused and showed no signs of being tired. He turned his attention back to Greta's house. *Fifty yards to go*, he thought.

Just then, as if shot forward by some magic force, Greta dashed ahead, her blond hair flying. She lengthened her lead with every stride. Chris bolted but he could not catch her. Greta reached her front lawn several strides ahead of him. The two stood on the frosted grass taking deep breaths of cold air. Greta stood with her hands on her hips. She looked down the street and saw Mingo bounding along, his leash slapping against the pavement as he went. Way behind Mingo, Mimi was still jogging at her steady pace.

"Did you come to kiss the winner, Mingo?" Greta asked as she knelt in front of her dog. As if on cue, Mingo happily licked Greta's face.

Chris rubbed his side, hoping to rub a sudden ache away. "I almost had you, Gretzky," he said, still breathing fast and deep.

Greta looked up from Mingo's happy licks. "Almost." She smiled.

ELEVEN

Phweeet!

Coach Anderson's whistle shrieked through the gymnasium. Within seconds, the balls stopped bouncing. Sneakers stopped squeaking. Everybody stopped talking and turned toward the coach.

"Scrimmage time!" Coach Anderson called with a broad grin.

The Eagles burst into cheers.

"All right!"

"Hoop time."

"Let's play some ball!"

Coach Anderson shouted out the lineups: "First team, Dontae Taylor, John Geraghty, Alan Weinberg, Andrew Mallamo, and Jonathan DeHart in blue. Second team, Brendan Buso, Chris Skallerup, Fasil Girmay, Jack Van Norden, and Jason Chun in gold. Full-court. Game to ten baskets."

"Do we still have to give those guys a four-basket lead?" Dontae asked as he dribbled the ball back and forth between his legs.

"Make it two baskets," Chris suggested. "We don't need four."

"Okay, two baskets," said the coach.

"Are you crazy, Chris?" Jason whispered as he turned his practice jersey to the gold side. "We need ten baskets against those guys. Who's gonna cover Dontae?"

"Don't worry," Chris said, pulling his shirt over his head. "I'll take him."

"All right, gold ball," Coach Anderson shouted, tossing Fasil the ball. "Both teams play half-court, man-to-man defense. Stay low, move your feet, and let's see some hustle."

The second team moved the ball around with sharp passes and quick cuts to the basket. Chris finally snapped a pass to Brendan, who buried an open jump shot.

"3–0, gold," called Coach Anderson. "Let's play some D, blue."

The blue team dribbled downcourt. Jonathan held up two fingers to signal a play and then passed to Dontae on the right wing. Chris leaned low in his defensive stance and stayed right with the Eagles star scorer. Dontae faked left and drove hard to the right, but Chris was not fooled by the fake. He had remembered Mimi's lessons. He concentrated on Dontae's hips instead of the ball and moved quickly to cut off Dontae's path to the basket. Dontae stopped dribbling and held the ball. Chris was on him, waving his arms wildly.

"Come on, move!" Dontae shouted impatiently as he looked for an open teammate.

The blue team kept moving and passing. Dontae got the ball again. This time he was in the middle of the floor, just past the foul line. Again Chris was right in front of him. Dontae faked a quick shot, lowered his shoulder, and dribbled to the left. Chris moved in front of Dontae. The two boys collided. Chris lost his balance and slid across the floor on the seat of his pants. Dontae tumbled over him.

Phweeet! Coach Anderson put his left hand in back of his head and pointed with his right to Dontae. "Foul on blue. Charging. Gold ball," he called.

Dontae smacked a flat palm against the floor. His eyes were angry and his lips were pressed tight together. He got up and moved into position but his expression didn't change.

Chris's dynamite defense had fired up the team. The second stringers gamely held on to their lead. Jason, Jack, and Brendan each sank jump shots. Even Chris faked Dontae off his feet and drove in for an easy basket.

"9–7. Gold!" Coach Anderson yelled after Chris's basket.

"Come on, blue!" Dontae shouted. "We need a bucket."

"Let's hold them, gold!" Chris shouted back. "Play D."

Jonathan dribbled down, held up two fingers, and passed the ball to Dontae on the right. The Eagles star forward tried to dribble to the basket, but Chris knocked the ball loose. The two players dove for the ball in a tangle of arms and elbows. Dontae's elbow cracked against Chris's jaw as the ball skidded out of bounds.

"Blue ball," Coach Anderson said.

Chris stood rubbing his sore chin as John Geraghty passed the ball inbounds. Alan Wienberg passed the ball to Dontae, who shoved his shoulder into Chris and dribbled hard to the hoop. Chris lost his balance for a moment and fell back. Dontae stopped and shot an off-balance jump shot. *Swish.*

"9–8. Gold team is still ahead," Coach Anderson called. "Game to ten."

"Nice foul," Chris said angrily to Dontae as the two boys ran downcourt.

"I didn't hear any whistle," Dontae shot back.

"Come on, gold!" Brendan yelled as the teams hustled downcourt. "One more basket and we win!" But the gold team could not put the game away.

Fasil missed a hook shot for the gold team and John Geraghty nailed a long jumper for the starters and knotted the score at 9–9.

"Next basket wins," Coach Anderson quickly

The two players dove for the ball in a tangle of arms and elbows.

reminded all the players.

The Eagles needed no reminders. They were breathing hard and their sweat-stained shirts stuck to their backs like a second skin. The gold team moved the ball around the blue team's clawing defense, and Jason passed to Chris in the corner. Chris faked a long shot and dribbled by a leaping Dontae for a short open jumper.

The ball felt good as it left Chris's hand, but it glanced off the front rim and rattled out.

Jonathan DeHart grabbed the rebound and dribbled upcourt, looking for the winning blue basket. He flicked a quick pass to Dontae in his favorite spot on the right side of the court. But Chris was right on him, crouching in his defensive stance.

Dontae dribbled right, but Chris stopped him. Dontae quickly looked around to pass. Chris stepped in, pressing him even closer. Dontae swung the ball around, still looking to pass. His left elbow caught Chris smack on the jaw. Chris's head snapped back.

"Hey, watch the elbows!" Chris shouted.

"Get out of my face, man!" Dontae snapped back.

Chris pushed even closer. The two boys were standing face to face, their eyes blazing.

Phweeet! Phweeet!!

"Cut it out, you two!" Coach Anderson said as he moved quickly to separate them. Dontae stepped back, the basketball now on his hip.

"That's enough of that," Coach Anderson said sharply.

The coach looked at Chris and Dontae. "Why don't you guys shake hands?"

Dontae looked at Chris and put out his hand. "Sorry about the elbows, man," he said.

"That's okay," Chris said, although he didn't mean it. He shook Dontae's hand and turned away.

Coach Anderson looked at the rest of the Eagles. "All right, that's enough for today. Hit the showers!" he said.

Chris stood for a moment in the middle of the floor, breathing slowly through his nose. The other members of the team filed out of the gym.

"Come on, Chris," Coach Anderson said. "You'd better get going."

Chris started to the door slowly. He was thinking about Dontae, the tie scrimmage, and the shot he had missed that could have won it all.

"Chris," Coach Anderson called. Chris turned around and faced his coach. The coach smiled. "Good defense," he said.

TWELVE

As Chris and Jason raced up the familiar stairs to the school gymnasium, they could hear basketballs and feet pounding louder and louder. When they reached the doors, they heard a voice rising above all the noise.

"Come on, Eagles. Let's go!"

"That's gotta be Mimi," Chris said to Jason as they passed Mr. Karavetsos, the seventh grade history teacher, at the gym doorway.

"You boys coming to see how the game should be played?" Mr. Karavetsos teased.

"Greta Pemberton's a friend," Chris explained.

Mr. Karavetsos nodded with approval and said, "She's a player."

Chris pointed to the stands as the two boys stepped inside. "There's Mimi," he said. "Let's sit with her." Chris and Jason walked along the edge of the floor where the two girls' teams were going through their pregame drills. They climbed over a couple of wooden benches and sat down behind the

Eagles bench. "Hey, Mimi," Chris said.

"Hey, Chris, good to see you," Mimi replied. "Who do you have with you?"

"Oh, this is Jason. He's one of the guys on the basketball team," Chris said.

"Hi, Jason."

"Hi, Mrs. Pemberton."

"Call me Mimi," she said quickly and turned her attention back to the floor.

The two teams were lining up for the tip-off, the Eagles in their blue and gold uniforms, the Wood Acres Wildcats in red.

"Which one is Lily Harris?" Jason asked.

"Number 14, the one with the red wristbands," Mimi answered without taking her eyes off the game. "And the pink fingernails."

"She's a big scorer," Chris said as he leaned forward to get a better look. "You know she gets about twenty points a game."

Mimi turned to the boys and smiled. "Greta's gonna cover her. Believe me, she won't score twenty points today."

Neither team scored much in the first half. Greta stuck to Lily Harris like a shadow, following her all over the court. Mimi nudged Chris during the first half and observed, "See how Greta is staying low in her defensive stance and moving her feet? Just like I've been teaching you."

70

Chris nodded as his eyes followed Greta. "Lily Harris is good, but she can't dribble by Greta at all," he said.

"That's because Greta noticed that Lily likes to dribble to the right all the time," Mimi said proudly. "Greta is playing her to that side and forcing her to dribble to the left."

Mimi looked at Chris and whispered, "That will be our next lesson."

Greta, of course, did not just play defense. Less than a minute before the end of the half, she streaked downcourt. She dribbled to the left, spun to the right, and leaped between two defenders, threading a shot between their outstretched arms. The ball touched off the glass backboard and fell through the net. Greta had tied the game 16-16! Seconds later, the buzzer blared long and loud. All the players looked up at the scoreboard, grabbed their water bottles, and headed to their locker rooms.

Chris, Jason, and Mimi were on their feet.

"What a move!" Chris shouted, throwing his hands into the air.

Later, as the teams warmed up for the second half, Chris and Jason reviewed the first half. "Tough game. The Wildcats look pretty good," Jason said.

"Yeah," Chris agreed. "But Gretzky is really doing a good job keeping the pressure on Lily Harris. I don't think she's even scored."

"But Greta hasn't scored that much either," Jason noted.

"Yeah, but did you see that amazing move at the end of the half?" Chris said as he imitated Greta's final shot.

The buzzer sounded again and the teams headed back to their benches. Greta winked at her mother as she trotted by. After huddling with their coaches, the players ran back onto the floor, clapping as they went.

"Go get 'em, Gretzky!" Chris shouted above the crowd.

The second half had hardly begun when Greta did just that. On the first possession she dribbled past two Wildcat defenders for a twisting layup.

Phweeet! The referee blew her whistle and moved her right hand down in a chopping motion. "The basket is good," she said. "Foul on red, number five. One shot."

Greta stepped to the foul line. She spun the ball in her hands and bounced it three times just as Chris had seen her do hundreds of times down at Green Street Park. The gym fell silent as Greta eyed the front rim, dipped, and shot.

Swish.

The Wildcats brought the ball downcourt. Lily Harris missed a jump shot. Sharon Hanley grabbed the rebound and tossed a perfect pass to Greta, who was sprinting ahead to the other basket. She caught the ball and, in one smooth motion, laid it up and in the basket.

Again the Wildcats brought the ball downcourt. Lily Harris dribbled confidently and looked for an open teammate. Greta moved in quickly and tipped the ball away from Lily. On the first bounce Greta got her palm on top of the ball and started dribbling furiously upcourt.

Lily, a bit stunned, managed to keep her wits and went flying after Greta. Just as Greta took a leap toward the basket, Lily leaped too. But quick-thinking Greta flipped the ball behind Lily's head to Erin Geraghty, who scored a basket for the Eagles.

The Wildcats coach shouted for a time-out. Only two minutes into the third quarter, the Eagles led 21–14.

The crowd was on its feet dancing and cheering.

"What a pass!"

"All right, Eagles!"

Mimi's voice rose above the noise of the crowd. "That's my girl!" she shouted with her fists thrust in the air. "That's my girl."

Greta shot her mother a look and mouthed *Mom!* as she walked to the Eagles bench for the time-out. Mimi mouthed back *Sorry* and quickly sat down.

"I know I promised not to yell at games," Mimi said to Chris as she continued to clap, "but I can't help it. I am so proud of her."

"I know. Moms are like that," said Chris.

The time-out did not help the Wildcats. Greta kept scoring and setting up her teammates for baskets. The Eagles kept stretching their lead.

With every basket, Mimi got more excited. But she kept her promise and stayed in her seat clapping until her hands turned red. "I didn't promise not to clap," she said to Chris.

The game ended with Greta dribbling around the Wildcats defense and firing a pass to Sharon for a final basket. Chris looked at the scoreboard as the buzzer went off.

The crowd made its way down to the floor. Mimi gave Greta a big hug as Chris and Jason looked on.

"Great game, Gretzky," Chris said. "You must have had twenty-five points."

"I don't know how many I had. But I know Lily Harris had only four points," Greta said, beaming with victory.

"Four points!" Jason said, laughing. "I didn't think she even had that many."

"When do you guys play the Wildcats?" Greta asked as she wiped her face with a towel.

"Saturday," Chris and Jason said in unison.

"Good luck."

"We'll need it," Chris said. "They've got that kid Tim Cooney who's unstoppable."

Mimi smiled confidently. "You can stop him," she said as she put her arm around Chris and looked over at her daughter. "You can stop anybody if you play good defense. Just stay low, move your feet, and keep hustling."

THIRTEEN

On Friday night, Chris's father leaned over the family's dining room table and wrote on a yellow piece of note paper. "Here is the Kopilow's number," he said. "We're going there for dinner. We should be home around 11:30."

Chris and his sister, Anna, nodded from the living room.

Their mother put on her coat and smoothed her hair in front of the mirror hanging in the front hall. "There's a pizza in the freezer that you can share," she said, still fussing with her hair.

"What kind?" Chris asked.

"Pepperoni," she answered and then nodded to the mirror as if finally satisfied with her look. "Just put it in the microwave. The instructions are on the box. Now, Chris, don't have too much soda. You know what that does to your stomach."

"Okay, okay," said Chris impatiently. He didn't like being reminded that soda made him burp a lot and he didn't want his mother to keep listing her rules for the evening.

But his mother continued: "Don't eat in the den. And clean up after yourselves. I don't want to come home to a sink full of dishes."

His parents moved toward the door. "We'll give you a call from the Kopilows," Mr. Skallerup said. "So Anna, don't tie up the phone talking with your friends."

"Good-bye, Dad. Good-bye, Mom," Anna said with a big pretend smile because she knew they could tell that she was really saying: *'Get going!'*

The parents laughed and walked out the door but their mother couldn't resist one last comment. "Be good," she said.

Anna leaned her hip into the door to shut it tight and then turned the dead bolt. "Do you want to eat now?" she asked Chris.

"Sure, I'm starving."

Anna set up the pizza in the microwave as Chris put ice in the glasses and poured the root beer. He poured it a little too quickly and it almost bubbled out onto the table.

"Don't drink too much soda, Chris, you know what it does to your stomach," Anna warned in a perfect imitation of their mother.

Chris smiled at his sister. As the bubbles settled down, he took a long gulp of soda, put his glass down and opened his mouth. *'Buuurrrrppp!'*

"Chris!" Anna screamed. "That is *so* gross."

77

"Thank you," Chris said, as he took a bow and came up grinning. "You know what soda does to my stomach."

Anna shook her head. When the pizza was ready they sat down to eat it. "You want two slices?" Anna asked.

"Sure."

"Watch out, it's hot."

Chris didn't listen to his sister. He took a big bite. It was so hot that his jaw automatically dropped open to let the heat out. Then he grabbed a quick swig of root beer to cool off his tongue.

"Don't you dare burp again, Chris!" Anna warned.

"Don't worry, my stomach's fine," Chris said, waving a hand in front of his open mouth. "It's my tongue. It's burning up."

"I told you it was hot," Anna said, quite pleased with herself.

As Chris waited for the pizza to cool, he talked with his sister: "Did your volleyball team play today?" he asked.

"Yeah."

"How'd you do?"

"We lost in four sets. It was 17–15 in the fourth set."

"Too bad. How did *you* do?" Chris asked as he bit into his pizza.

"Pretty good. I had a great save," Anna said,

beginning to get excited at the memory. "The ball was going way off the court and I leaped and knocked back a perfect set for Tamika."

"Did you get any spikes this game?"

"Will you quit asking me that, Chris? I keep telling you, that's not my job on the team."

"Yeah, but don't you ever wish you could get a chance to spike it?" Chris asked, wiping some sauce from his chin with the back of his hand.

"Sure, I'd love to be a star." Anna shrugged. "But I'm not that tall. I'm only 5 feet 5 inches."

"Five feet $4\frac{1}{2}$ inches," Chris corrected her quickly. "I'm 5 feet 5 inches."

"All right, *little* brother, 5 feet $4\frac{1}{2}$. But anyway, my job is to set up Tamika and Sarah." Anna took another slice of pizza, popping a loose pepperoni into her mouth. "Wouldn't you like to be the high scorer on your basketball team?"

"Sure." Chris nodded. "Except I can't shoot."

"I thought Greta was helping you."

"She is."

"Aren't you getting better?"

"A little bit," Chris answered, thinking back on his many practice sessions. "But I still can't shoot like Gretzky. She's awesome." Chris grabbed the final slice of pizza and kept talking. "Did I tell you that her mom is teaching me how to play better defense?"

"No," Anna said, looking surprised. "What does her mom know about playing basketball?"

"A lot," Chris answered. "She played six-on-six basketball when she was in high school in Iowa. She was a defender and couldn't cross the center-court line."

"Oh, yeah. I've heard about that. How are the lessons going?"

"Real good. Mimi is cool," Chris said. "And I figure if I get really good at playing defense, Coach Anderson will play me more in the games."

"Kind of like me setting up Sarah and Tamika instead of spiking," Anna said as she flashed a triumphant smile.

"Yeah, I guess," Chris said. Chris knew Anna was right but did not want to admit it to her.

Anna pushed back her chair and started to clear her dishes. "Well, are you any good at defense?" she asked.

"Yeah. I shut down Dontae at our last practice," Chris said. "He's the highest scorer on the team."

"You must be pretty good," Anna said as she turned away from the table. She opened the dishwasher and put her plate in.

Chris smiled as he looked at his sister. "You know what else I'm good at?" he asked and then took a long last gulp of root beer.

"No, what?"

Chris waited until his sister had turned around and was looking right at him. He opened his mouth wide and...

"*Buuurrrrppp.*"

FOURTEEN

Chris and Jason were sitting on the end of the bench. Chris leaned back as Jason reached over for another cup of water.

"Hey, cut it out," Chris warned. "You don't want to play with a bunch of water sloshing around in your belly."

"So what?" Jason said, slurping down the last drops from the cup. "This game's too close. We're never gonna get in."

Chris looked up at the scoreboard. The Eagles trailed the Wood Acres Wildcats by two points.

On the court, the Wildcats star player, Tim Cooney, dribbled downcourt with Dontae right on him. On the bench, Chris thought: *Get your rear end down, Dontae, you're not staying low on defense.*

In an instant, Cooney switched his dribble to his left hand and blew by Dontae for a basket.

"Come on, let's play some defense!" Coach Anderson shouted. "Cut him off."

Andrew Mallamo missed a shot for the Eagles. Cooney grabbed the rebound, raced downcourt, and canned a quick jumper. Suddenly the Eagles were down by six.

"No way Dontae can stay with Cooney," Jason whispered to Chris.

"He can do it," Chris disagreed. Chris pointed to the floor as Cooney dribbled downcourt against the Eagles. "Dontae's just got to get into good defensive position. He keeps reaching out with his hands and trying to stop Cooney that way. He's got to move his feet and get in front of him."

Just then, Cooney faked right and spun to the left, leaving Dontae off-balance and grasping nothing but air. Cooney's short jumper swished through the net.

Coach Anderson stomped an angry foot on the floor. Chris leaned forward and looked down the bench, hoping the coach would put him in. When the Eagles dribbled past the bench, Chris got his wish.

"Chris!" Coach Anderson shouted. Chris bolted

from the end of the bench and was standing next to his coach almost before his name was out of the coach's mouth.

"Go in for Dontae next time-out," the coach instructed. "You get Cooney, number fifteen. And stick with him."

The horn sounded and Chris trotted onto the court. Dontae walked by, out of breath. "I had Cooney, number fifteen," he said, shaking his head. "Good luck, he's real tough."

Jonathan DeHart dribbled to the foul line and passed to Chris. He passed up an open shot at the basket and flicked a pass to John Geraghty, who sank a jumper from the corner. The Eagles trailed, 24–18.

The Wildcats quickly got the ball to Cooney on the wing. Chris crouched low in his defensive position just a few feet away as Mimi had taught him. Cooney faked to the right with his head and shoulders and then drove left. But he did not fool Chris, who slid over and cut off his path to the basket. Cooney stopped dribbling and held the ball over his head. Chris reached up and tipped the ball loose.

"Blue ball!" the referee called as the ball bounced off Cooney's leg and out of bounds. Coach Anderson jumped off the Eagles bench. "All right. Good D!"

Andrew sank a running hook shot to cut the

Wildcats lead to four, 24–20.

"Hold the ball for the last shot," the Wildcats coach told his team from the bench.

Chris glanced at the clock. *Ten seconds left in the half,* he thought. *They'll try to get it to Cooney.*

Sure enough, the Wildcats point guard whistled a sharp pass toward the star scorer. Chris was ready. He pounced, stretched, and tipped the ball to midcourt as time ran out. The Eagles bench and their fans were on their feet as the team came off the floor. Jason clapped Chris on the back and shouted happily, "All right! The end of the bench is coming through."

"Way to play defense," called a familiar voice. Chris saw Mimi standing and pumping her fist in the air. Greta reached over and pulled her mother back down to her seat.

Coach Anderson gathered his team just before the second half for a pep talk. "Only four down, guys. We can do it. We'll start the second half with the regular starters. Dontae, you've gotta keep Cooney under control."

But within minutes, the Eagles were down by eight points. At the end of the bench, Jason took another cup of water and whispered to Chris, "Coach has gotta put you on Cooney again. You're the only guy who can stop him."

Just then, Cooney sank another jumper.

"Chris!" Coach Anderson called.

Chris popped off the bench. "Go in for Andrew, but you cover Cooney. Tell Dontae to take Andrew's man. Okay?"

Chris nodded and thought, *There's plenty of time left, we can still come back.*

The Eagles traded baskets with the Wildcats for the rest of the quarter. Chris smothered Cooney on defense but the Eagles could not pull any closer. The lead was still ten as the two teams got ready for the final quarter.

Coach Anderson knelt before his team and pleaded. "Come on, we're only down by ten. We're still in it, but we've gotta play better defense and rebound better."

"Are the same guys who finished the third quarter gonna start the fourth?" Jonathan asked.

"No, we're gonna make a couple of substitutions."

Chris looked at his coach, hoping he would not be taken out of the game.

"Brendan and Fasil go in for Alan and John. Chris, you stay in and cover Cooney. We've gotta stop him. Let's go."

Chris walked onto the court thinking about Mimi's lessons on defense. *Stay low. Move your feet. Keep hustling.* Slowly the Eagles picked away at the Wildcats lead. Chris's defense forced Cooney to take a series of off-balance shots. Only one of

Cooney's shots fell in, while the rest rolled off the rim. Baskets by Brendan and Dontae edged the Eagles closer.

With less than one minute left, Chris hustled downcourt, outrunning Cooney to take a perfect pass from Jonathan for a layup. He looked at the scoreboard as he ran downcourt. *42–40. We're only down by two*, he thought, his heart pounding from the excitement.

"Gotta hold them!" Coach Anderson yelled above the cheers of the Eagles bench.

The Wildcats passed the ball around as the game wound down. The Eagles were tired but they got a burst of energy and moved in aggressively, yelling instructions to one another.

"Pick up number twenty."

"I got him. I got him."

"Pick left. Go through."

The crowd was going wild. With twenty seconds to go, the Wildcats passed to Cooney on the left wing. Wide-eyed and breathless, Chris stood in his defensive stance just a few feet away.

"I got him!" he shouted to his teammates.

Cooney drove hard to the basket, sending up a shot that would have put the game out of reach. But Chris leaped and blocked the shot with the very tips of his fingers. The teams rushed after the ball in a mad scramble. Dontae scooped the ball up and

*But Chris leaped and blocked the shot
with the very tips of his fingers.*

dribbled desperately toward the Eagles basket. Two Wildcats players surrounded him and forced him to pass to Chris, who was sprinting from behind, trying to catch up to the play.

"Five...four...three..." the entire Eagles bench counted down.

With no time to dribble or pass, Chris could only shoot. Pointing his shoulders to the basket and keeping his elbow in, Chris sent a long three pointer spinning to the basket.

"Two...one..."

It's got a chance, Chris thought as the ball sailed straight for the basket. But the ball just touched the edge of the front rim, knocked off the back rim and bounced away. Chris stood on the floor in despair and disbelief as the buzzer sounded and the Wildcats celebrated. The Eagles comeback had fallen two points short: 42–40.

Parents and friends filled the floor after the teams shook hands. Chris's mother gave him a hug and his father said, "You played a great game. You almost had them."

"Yeah, almost," Chris said, managing a weak smile.

Greta and her mother walked by. "Good game, Chris," Greta called. "I'll see you at the park."

"You played great defense, Chris," Mimi added.

Chris nodded and then looked at the floor. *I can't believe that last shot didn't go in*, he thought. *It felt great.*

"I know you didn't win," said his sister, Anna, trying to console him. "But at least you played more. And you played really well."

Coach Anderson overheard Anna and said: "If Chris keeps playing defense like that, he'll be playing a lot more, that's for sure." The coach slapped his hand on Chris's sweaty shoulder and quickly pulled it back. "You'd better get out of this drafty gym and into the showers," he said.

For the first time since he missed the final shot, Chris really smiled. As he trotted off to the locker room he was still smiling.

FIFTEEN

The next morning, Chris stood at the top of the hill at Green Street Park. Along the edge of the park, bare tree limbs reached up and scratched at the clear blue sky.

Below, a lone figure bounced a basketball. A black dog romped near the chain-link fence of the empty tennis courts.

Chris made his way slowly down the hill, remembering how weeks before he had come to the park and asked Greta to help him and how that had changed everything. The snow was gone now and the hill was covered with the yellowed grasses of late winter. Chris scampered down the last part of the slope. "Hey, Gretzky!" Chris shouted when he reached the bottom.

Greta turned and smiled. "I was wondering if you would come down today."

"I guess I'm getting to be as crazy as you."

"You want another shooting lesson?" Greta asked.

"I'd better practice my last-second three-point jump shot," Chris laughed.

Greta passed Chris the ball and started to count down. "Three...two...one..."

Chris dribbled and lofted a long jump shot into the air. This time, the ball sailed straight and true, right through the net.

Swish.

"*Now* I make it," Chris cried, throwing his arms out wide in mock anger.

"Your shot in the game was a good shot," Greta said. "You almost made it."

"Almost," Chris said.

The two friends moved about the court, shooting and talking. "You got a lot of playing time yesterday," Greta said as she sank a long jump shot.

"Yeah," Chris agreed. "Coach must have played me half the game."

"Were you getting tired at the end?"

Chris shook his head as he grabbed one of Greta's rare missed shots. "No. I guess running with you and your mom is getting me into shape."

"Then I guess we'll keep running." Greta smiled.

Chris swished a short jump shot and Greta snapped back a pass.

"Good, because the Coach said he's gonna play me more." Chris's shot bounced off the rim and into Greta's hands.

"Maybe you'll start making more of your shots," Greta teased.

"That would be nice." Chris laughed. "But I think the coach is playing me because he really likes my defense."

"My mom said you played great defense against Cooney," Greta reported. "You kept low, kept moving your feet. She said were a good student. She gave you an A+."

"Your mom's a good teacher."

Greta shot a long jumper from past the foul line. *Swish.*

Chris got the ball from under the basket. Greta stood past the foul line with her hands out for the ball. Chris walked out a few steps, flipped the ball to Greta, and then got into his defensive stance. "Let's see how good a student I am," he said. "Come on, try and score on me."

Greta's eyes widened. "Okay," she said softly, as if she had been waiting for Chris to dare her.

Greta faked a shot, but Chris did not fall for the fake. She dribbled to the right, then drove to the left, sending the ball between her legs from her right hand to her left hand. Chris stayed right with her every step. Greta stopped with her back to the basket and spun to the left. Chris, certain that she was about to shoot, moved in to block the shot. But at the last instant, Greta spun back to the right, slid by Chris, and put up an off-balance, right-handed scoop shot.

*But at the last instant, Greta spun back to the right, slid by
Chris, and put up an off-balance, right-handed scoop shot.*

Chris turned and watched the ball glance off the backboard and just roll off the rim. He snatched away the rebound.

"Man, what a move!" he said to Greta with admiration. "I can't believe you almost made that shot."

"Almost," Greta said, her voice edged with disappointment. She eyed Chris. "I guess you are a pretty good student," she admitted.

Greta held out her hands and asked, "How about giving me another shot?"

Chris tossed her the ball and got low into his defensive stance. This time, Greta faked left and dribbled right lofting a long, running hook shot over Chris's outstretched hand. The ball plunked off the backboard and angled through the hoop. The net danced in the sun.

Chris grabbed the ball and Greta jogged to her position past the foul line.

"I don't want you thinking that just 'cause you can stop Tim Cooney," she said, looking straight at Chris, "you can stop me, too."

Chris laughed. "Let's keep playing," he said as he bounced the ball to Greta. "And we'll see if I can stop you."

The End

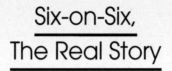

Six-on-Six,
The Real Story

Basketball was created as a game for rowdy young men. It was invented in 1891 by James Naismith, who had just taken over an unruly physical education class at a YMCA school in Springfield, Massachusetts. It was December, and Naismith knew the young men would not be satisfied with merely playing leapfrog in the gym through the long winter months. He needed to come up with a new game.

Within days Naismith came up with the perfect indoor game for his wild bunch, and the only equipment he used was a ball and a peach basket nailed to the balcony of the gym. He called the game *basket ball* (two words), and it was very similar to the version of the game played today (although dribbling was not allowed).

In 1895, Clara Baer, a college physical education teacher in New Orleans, adapted the rules of *basket ball* to make them more "suitable" for women. She gave her game a frilly name—*basquette*—and said it was just right for a "a delicate girl, unaccustomed to exercise." Baer thought the men's game was too rough, and she didn't want the women running full court because she thought it would put too much strain on their hearts! She therefore divided the court into sections to limit players' movement around the court. A player had to stay in her designated playing area on the court and was not allowed

1927 Iowa State College students practicing guarding and passing.

to play into another section. She had to pass the ball to move it out of her playing area.

Baer's version of basketball developed into the six-on-six game that was played by girls and women for more than 75 years. It was named "six-on-six" because there were six players on each team.

Three girls on each team played only offense while the other three played only defense (like Greta's mom). No girl could cross the center-court line: offensive players played on one half of the court, and defensive players stayed on the other half. If any girl reached the center line, she had to stop and pass the ball to one of her teammates to get it to the other side of the court.

The girls' game may have started out as a gentler version of the boys', but it eventually became a hard-charging, high-scoring game. Players specialized in either offense or defense. It was easy for offensive players to shoot and score many times because only three defensive players (who were restricted in their defensive actions) were allowed on the half of the court with the basket.

Six-on-six girls basketball (which was played at some schools until 1993) was more popular in the state of Iowa in the 1960s—where the girls played wild, heart-pounding games—than anywhere else. The Iowa girls' six-on-six state high school basketball tournament was played before packed crowds of up to 15,000 fans every year. The girls' tournament was even more popular than the boys' tournament. In Iowa, it was said that little boys dreamed of playing basketball like their mothers and sisters.

Heywood Hale Broun, a famous sportswriter who covered sports events ranging from the

Kentucky Derby to the Super Bowl, claimed that the Iowa girls' six-on-six tournament was the most thrilling sports competition he had ever seen. "It was sport at its best," said Broun. "Full of joy and zest and excitement."

The 1968 girls' championship game was televised in nine states and was the stuff of legends. Union-Whitten edged Everly in overtime in a 113-107 shoot-out. Denise Long led Union-Whitten with 64 points.

Denise Long, Union-Whitten, launching a jump shot in the 1968 Iowa Girls High School State Tournament.

She was later drafted by the San Francisco Warriors, an all-men's NBA team (there were no professional women's teams in 1968), although she never played for them. And Denise Long was

99

not even the championship game's high scorer. Jeanette Olson of Everly poured in 76 points for the losing team.

Iowa girls' basketball was loaded with high-scoring forwards. The all-time national amateur scoring leader (of both women's *and* men's amateur basketball) is Lynne Lorenzen, a six-on-six star who played for Ventura High School (1983-1987) in Iowa. Lorenzen scored 6,736 points in her years at Ventura and averaged more than 60 points a game.

Today, women don't have to join the NBA to play professional basketball. Women play in their own professional leagues. And the rules are the same as the men's. When we see the stars of women's basketball today—Sheryl Swoopes, Rebecca Lobo, and Lisa Leslie, to name a few—going full court, it's hard to imagine that anybody ever thought women were too fragile to play "men's" basketball.

Acknowledgments

The author would like to thank Mr. Troy Dannen of the Iowa Girls High School Athletic Union for providing information about Iowa women's six-on-six basketball. Much of the information about six-on-six basketball and Iowa women's basketball found in The Real Story chapter is from *Basketball, a History of the Game* by Alexander Wolff, and from *From Six-On-Six to Full Court Press, A Century of Iowa Girls' Basketball* by Janice A. Beran.

About the Author

One of the biggest disappointments of Fred Bowen's life was that he did not make his high school varsity basketball team in Marblehead, Massachusetts. But he did not stop playing. Mr. Bowen played pickup basketball and in recreational leagues for twenty-five years. He played on one team, the Court Jesters, for eighteen straight seasons.

Now Mr. Bowen coaches a kids' basketball team. In fact, he has been coaching the same kids for the past eight years —since they were in the first grade.

Mr. Bowen, author of *T.J.'s Secret Pitch, The Golden Glove, The Kid Coach, Playoff Dreams,* and *Full Court Fever,* lives in Silver Spring, Maryland, with his wife and two children.

HEY, SPORTS FANS!
Have We Got Spectacular News For You!

Announcing...

The AllStar SportStory Series
Fan Club!

A fun way to learn more about these action-packed sports books that mix stories about regular kids playing ball with real sports history. We'll also tell you more about the author Fred Bowen (who's the biggest sports fan!) and his plans for upcoming books in the series.

When you join the club, we'll send you some really cool stuff...

★ An AllStar SportStory Series Fan Club newsletter filled with great sports facts, quizzes, stories, and everything there is to know about these sports books

★ A book sticker autographed by author Fred Bowen

★ An AllStar SportStory series ball card (a perfect bookmark!)

★ A fan club membership card

Here's how you join...

1. Put your name, address, and a first-class stamp on a legal-sized envelope.

2. Ask your parents for a money order or check for $1.00 made payable to Peachtree Publishers (for shipping and handling). *Do not send cash in the mail.*

3. Tear out the form below and fill it out.

4. Put everything in an envelope and send it to:

The AllStar SportStory Series Fan Club
Peachtree Publishers
494 Armour Circle NE
Atlanta, GA 30324

(And, if you want, you can also send a letter to author Fred Bowen!)

— — — — — — — — — — — — — — — —

Your Name _____ Age _____

Your Address _____

City _____ State _____ Zip _____

Your School _____

Your Favorite AllStar SportStory Book _____

(Please allow 4–6 weeks for delivery)

Book Seven in the
AllStar SportStory Series—

THE FINAL CUT

Four friends trying out for the school basketball team have a hard time competing against each other.

With each tryout they wonder: Who will make the final cut, and how will it affect their friendship?

Look for Fred Bowen's
THE FINAL CUT
coming Spring 1999!